GOLDEN BOOKS & DESIGN,™ A GOLDEN BOOK,® and
the distinctive gold spine are trademarks of Golden Books Publishing Company, Inc.

A GOLDEN BOOK®
Golden Books Publishing Company, Inc.
New York, New York 10106
No part of this book may be reproduced or copied in any form without
written permission from the copyright owner. Produced in U.S.A.

Draw some flowers.

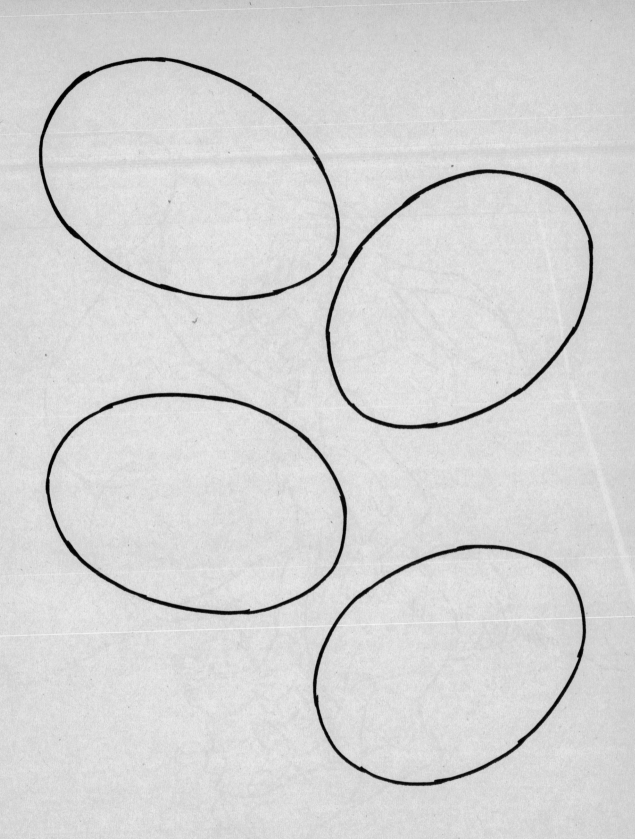

Decorate the Easter eggs.

How old are you?
Draw that many candles on the cake.

Trace the clouds.
What shapes do they make?

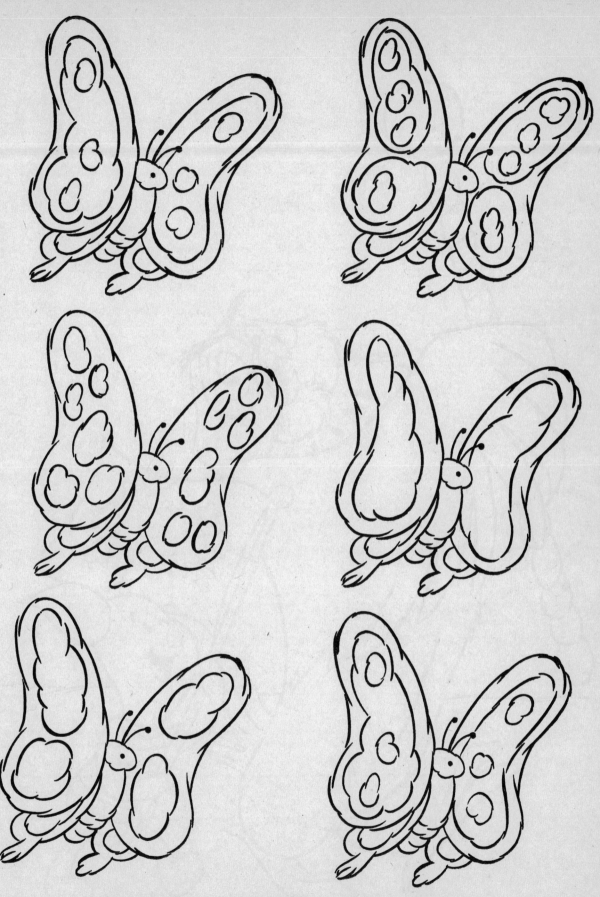

Find the matching butterflies.

What is your favorite time of year?
Draw something you like to do then.